R.S. HASPIEL

A SHORT STORY BY R.S. HASPIEL

PASSIONATE IMPROPRIETY

A VICTORIAN LOVE STORY

authorHOUSE®

AuthorHouse™
1663 Liberty Drive
Bloomington, IN 47403
www.authorhouse.com
Phone: 1 (800) 839-8640

Published by AuthorHouse 10/11/2019

ISBN: 978-1-7283-3011-2 (sc)
ISBN: 978-1-7283-3119-5 (hc)
ISBN: 978-1-7283-3010-5 (e)

Library of Congress Control Number: 2019915540

Print information available on the last page.

Any people depicted in stock imagery provided by Getty Images are models, and such images are being used for illustrative purposes only.
Certain stock imagery © Getty Images.

Cover Artist: Victoria Cooper

This book is printed on acid-free paper.

This book may not have been written for Marie but certainly embodies her spirit and her soul. For you my love.

CHAPTER 1

THE OLD VICTORIAN MANOR LOOKED COLDER THAN USUAL as Eleanor walked out to survey her old homestead. Four years ago she was happily embroiled in the hustle of London traffic and thought she would gradually wear down her brothers' business partners into accepting the mysterious character she had become. Her odd way of dressing placed her in the same eccentric company as George Sand, yet her knowledge and sense for business made those who were close to her never stray too far. For Eleanor was one of the few whom making money through business ventures came easily. E.B. Randhorne was the talk of the town for a while when his decision to purchase several goods from China turned into mass appeal with the wealthy society ladies. Silks and brightly colored textiles we the rage as well as Laudanum. The slightly alcoholic mixture worked as a painkiller and relaxant. Reinvestment into several shipping lines to the Americas had solidified her brothers' position in the Queensbury Men's Club and made E.B. Randhorne a financial force to be reckoned with. Such new clipper ship purchases were bound to increase E.B. Randhorne's wealth substantially. The Sovereign of the Seas, The Golden West and the Ocean Chief to the Americas all brought trade goods to the new British markets. But the most popular of the new trade were the Opiates. Preparations that had Opium in them were marketed towards women.

Eleanor thought it amusing that E.B. Randhorne had never been to the club personally but was accepted for membership almost immediately upon her brothers' request. What a fright it would cause to have Eleanor Barton Randhorne of Heddington at the Queensbury Men's Club. While she thought the revelation an amusing prospect she would never knowingly place her dear brother at risk to public humiliation and banishment; so for the time being only a few well chosen friends were privy to the true identity of the wealthy E.B. Randhorne.

Eleanor's occasional appearances among the ladies society, which was held at the Whitehall Inn, were polite and subdued for her nature. Her unusual dress was merely passed off as that of a Bohemian style artist. But only she could turn their idle chatter regarding their husband's jobs into useful business knowledge. E.B. Randhorne would soon be in the local gossip again. How old was this E.B. Randhorne and whom would he marry? Some of the ladies even discussed using the new Chloroform mixture given to them by their dentists. One of the ladies husbands had Waterloo teeth which were real human teeth that were attached to hand carved ivory and used as dentures. Eleanor preferred not to think of the poor sod who sold his teeth or worse yet dying and having his teeth pulled and made into this dental monstrosity. As she removed herself from the next level of gossip she eyed a young woman in the lobby of the inn. Not only was she carrying her own luggage but was traveling alone according to her own admission to the desk clerk. Her mode of dress was as eccentric as Eleanor's. A silken shirt worn loosely was like that of a mans. Her long grey skirt barely brushed the floor and no bustle was present as she turned her back toward me. After spending hours with the ladies social and trying desperately not to fall asleep I was intrigued by this breath of fresh air. She was told to be seated whilst a higher authority was sought with regards to her reservation.

Clearly she was not here for the ladies social hour. I made my apologies and removed myself from the ladies circle. Quietly, I lit one of my small cigars and sat within earshot of this new visitor. As expected, the proprietor of the hotel seemed to have difficulty accommodating her. He asked her several times if she was escorted by anyone, since young single ladies did not venture out alone unless they were of questionable morals. She explained to him in a calm yet slightly irritated voice that she was a noted archeologist and was staying as a guest at the Fairfax Hotel but that she was asked to leave due to her inappropriate manner of dress. Her irritation was now clearly visible as she stood to confront the proprietor. I feared that an altercation was soon to follow so I put out my forbidden cigar and decided to intervene. *"Forgive the intrusion Mr. Brumby but I couldn't help but overhear the fact that your inn is full. Is that correct?"* The proprietor busily looked at his book as he spoke. *"Ahh…yes. That is correct Lady Heddington."* I had to stifle a smile as I was about to rescue a damsel in distress. *"Mr. Randhhorne's reservation is still standing….is it not?"* He grumbled as he checked his book once more. *"Why……of course! We always keep a vacancy for him."* I turned and smiled at the young woman and gave her a quick wink. *"Well, Mr. Randhorne will not be requiring his room this weekend as he is in Cornwall, so as you can see, you now have a vacancy. I'm sure this young lady would take the room?"* The proprietor was clearly caught off guard. We both noticed his flustered look and behavior and tried to stifle the laughter that was slowly creeping forward with every frustrated movement he made. *"We shall be in the dining room while you see to Mrs…….."* I eagerly awaited a name to go with the most exquisite face. *"It's Professor….Professor Rebecca*

Almonte." "*While you see to Professor Almonte's luggage and room.*" As she picked up her briefcase I escorted the professor into the dining room where we proceeded to contain our laughter no longer. "*I have never been so irritated yet so wonderfully amused in my life. And whom do I have to thank for this wonderful intervention? Mr. Randhorne or.....Lady Heddington?*" I took out my cigars and politely offered her one. I was not surprised when she confidently took one. "*Lady Eleanor Heddington at your service. I take it by your calm demeanor that this is not the first time you have encountered the Brumby's of this world?*" I tried not to watch her too intently as her lips caressed the tip of the cigar. I held out the match as she lit her cigar and gently held my hand as she blew out the flame. "*I fail to see what the issue is amongst English society. I've traveled to continents where having two wives is the norm ! Did you know that there are cultures where clothes are optional?*" She took several puffs and gazed out the small curtained window in front of our table. The waiter delivered a teapot, two teacups with saucers and a plate of warmed scones. "*How do you cope with it?*" Her question was asked in earnest as she chose her pastry. "*I mean.....your word is obviously listened to around here as evidence by Mr. Brumbys actions and you are a woman whose manner of dress, which I admire by the way, doesn't exactly fit the norm. So how do you do it?*" I chose my words carefully, wanting to tell her all yet realizing that I too had to be careful in my responses. *"Well....to begin with....my residence is not here at the Whitehall Inn. I reside at Hedgewick Manor. I induldge in the English Ladies Society to keep abreast of business events and investment opportunities through the local gossip."* I poured some tea, put out my cigar and took a bite of a luscious cream filled scone. *"But what good does that knowledge do you when you are not permitted to use it? I mean....at least without a husband."* I couldn't help but stifle a laugh. *"Let us say that I know of a gentleman that handles my investments and handles them based on what I tell him."* While her dress may have been slightly masculine her manner was anything but that. Her poise and demeanor was very lady like even to the sipping of afternoon tea. *"Let me guess....your benefactor would be Mr. Randhorne?"* *"Yes...that would be him. But I'm not sure how much pull he has with Mr. Brumby."* She stared into her empty cup. *"I never dreamed that finding a suitable place to do my research would be so damned difficult."* I poured her some more tea. *"And what type of research would that be?"* She reached down into her briefcase and pulled out a stack of clipped pages of notes and scraps of paper. *"The ruins at Westmore. I've worked three years on that site and have some definite provable theories. My evidence to support my theory came just this past week and...."* As she continued we were suddenly interrupted by Mr. Brumby. *"Madame.....Lady Heddington? I'm afraid I can only permit a one night stay. My guests would not take kindly to my establishment permitting a single woman to reside here. I'm terribly sorry.*" With that said he grumbled and had the man at the desk resume his duties. "*Well….I guess that settles that.*" She sipped her tea and once again fell silent as she gazed out the window. She looked lost as she placed her papers back into her suitcase. "*What is it exactly that you require for this research?*" I watched her as she ran her fingers over her silky brown hair. Her beautiful blue eyes scanned the table as she organized her thoughts. "*What I require? Well…..walking distance to a library, a typewriter and some peace and quiet. I ask you…..would that have been so terrible and scandalous?*" I smiled as I spoke, "*Perhaps I can offer you a suitable alternative…right down to the historical library since I'm assuming that is what you would need.*" "*I wouldn't wish to inconvenience you….I…I've imposed too much as it is.*" I stood up and placed several coins on the table. "*You may stay at Hedgewick Manor. Its library is quite substantial and comes complete with an American typewriter. There is only the housekeeper Mrs. Potter, the cook and myself along with two strutting peacocks, two stable hands and several horses. The quiet is at times deafening.*" I watched for a reaction but could not tell whether mine was a favorable suggestion. "*I would not wish to impose on your benefactor Mr. Randhorne.*" I tried not to appear irritated as I spoke, *My dear Professor Almonte, I own*

Hedgewick Manor. Mr. Randhorne resides elsewhere as English etiquette and propriety dictates. So as you can see....whom I choose to invite as my guest is solely up to me." She could sense my irritation but smiled anyway. *"Very well then....It appears as though you will have a guest until my assistants arrive."* I summoned my carriage, had Professor Almonte's luggage loaded and escorted her to the manor.

Our ride was a relatively quiet one with my mentioning periodic landmarks along the way. I tried not to be obvious in watching her but her independent manner and self assurance was very new and refreshing to me. As we passed the yellow flowered mustard fields I caught her looking at me. We both smiled politely and continued to look out the window. *"What beautiful horses in that field."* As I looked I noticed we had passed the first marker of my property. *"Glad you like them. Perhaps we can go riding sometime before your assistants arrive."* She smiled and looked at me with those enchanting eyes. *"Why? Are those your horses?"* I smiled back. *"Yes, as a matter of fact they are."*

As the carriage pulled up to the circular entrance I watched as the peacocks flew down off the stone wall that faced the driveway. *"What magnificent creatures!"* She said as she leaned forward to study the scenery. *"You won't think they're so magnificent after you've had one scream overhead as they fly down on top of you."* The carriage learched forward as she lost her balance and fell towards me. The scent of her now golden brown hair was like that of fresh roses. "*Sorry….I got a bit carried away. What a truly marvelous place* !" The door flew open as the groomsman offered his gloved hand as balance. My servants were lined up in the entryway as I walked towards Mrs. Potter. Had I been gone that long? The slow and gradual building of E.B. Randhorne's business ventures had taken me away from Hedgewick for long periods of time. Whilst I enjoyed the travel I longed for some peace and solitude. "*Good day mum. We didn't expect you back so soon. I'll have your room ready shortly.*" I turned to see the professor gathering in my paintings and tapestries. "*Mrs. Potter…..This is Professor Rebecca Almonte. She will be staying with us for a while. Please see to it that she is made comfortable during her stay.*" "*Yes mum.*" I interrupted Rebecca's gazing as I stood in front of her. "*Mrs. Potter will show you to your room so you can freshen up. I'll wait for you in the study. It's right down that hallway to your left.*" With that said she was off to get acquainted with Mrs. Potter. I headed towards the study which also housed an extensive library and thought I should do some tidying of my own. I sat behind my desk and looked at the open diary. It was nearly full; full of my hellish, nightmarish descriptions of brutal events and accidents. I closed the diary and placed the quill pen back in its cradle. I was not sure why I continued to document my nightmares, was it a search for answers or simply a desire for night time sanity?

Whatever the reason, my guest would not be privy to it and so I closed it. *"Your home is quite beautiful. And this library.....it certainly rivals any I have seen short of my university."* Rebecca looked around in total awe of the cavernous library before her. *"Thank you. Please.....sit down."* I never thought much about the library and how it must look to others. It's massive cherry shelves and ornately carved columns held volumes of leather bound books from Darwin and H.G. Wells to copies of local church records and their history. The winding staircase that led to the second story of the library allowed one to see the entire room as well as giving access to the more rare and unusual editions. I was somewhat proud of the fact that my collections also included certain books that had been banned. I kept those in a locked case upstairs towards the very end of the library. *"Good Lord! You even have Thomas Babington Macaulay and Thomas Carlyle."* She stood back up again and walked over to several books sitting on a table by the fireplace. *"Sartor Resartus? Did you know this book is banned in some areas?" "Why on earth would* The Tailor Retailored *be banned? I mean he did borrow some things from the German idealist philosophy but..."* She sat back down and answered. *"I believe it was in his response to views on England's social problems. They say it is quite vehement and written in his usual idiosyncratic style." "Well then...I guess you will simply have to read it yourself and come to your own conclusion."* As Rebecca continued to look around I continued. *"I realize that part of your research will be in the field but please feel free to use this as your home away from home. The archeology and research sections are down below and the more private collections are above."* Mrs. Potter gently knocked on the library door. As she entered she held a small piece of paper the size of a telegram. As I read it I knew it would require my presence back in the city. I watched as Rebecca caressed several leather bound editions of Jules Verne as though they were precious jewels. Her eyes were wide with exploration and wonderment. I wished I could have stayed to watch her explore further but my investments needed to be attended to. *"I'm afraid I must leave you for a few days. It seems Mr. Randhorne needs to conduct some business which I must assist him with. Please forgive me? I am, however, leaving you in the capable hands of Mrs. Potter. She might even be able to put you in touch with some locals for excavating purposes."* "Thank you......but *I fear your library has seduced me. I shall be here for several days at least."* Mrs. Potter smiled and spoke. *"Well....I hope miss will excuse herself for meals!"* I smiled as I made arrangements with Mrs. Potter and left Rebecca to her devices.

Once again E.B. Randhorne was making financial news. Two more Clipper ships of the extreme type were purchased from China and several items from the Orient, including the popular Opiate, were making an impact on English society. This Opiate was produced from the drying resin of unripe poppies and is used as a form of pleasure and medicinal forms. Since a treaty had been formed with China it opened up additional trading ports within the country. The ships Randhorne purchased were topsail brigantines, heavily sparred and canvased with sharply raking masts, low-sided and sharp bowed hulls and a rather deep draft which was greatest at the heel of the rudder. While the displacement was moderate for the hull dimensions the cargo carried was usually very small. These ships were the fastest of their type and could be used to transport small amounts of cargo at record speeds to most coastal destinations. A third bank account had to be opened for further ship purchases and New World business ventures. I had visited some of the Opium dens in China and found them to be dark, dank holes with every manner of being laying on anything from old mattresses to wooden slats on bricks. The small Chinese community that settled in London's docks brought with them the same obsession with Opium as I had observed back in China.

The streets of London were their usual crowded sea of humanity. My carriage could barely move amidst the vegetable wagons and flower stands. I had the driver stop and I walked the rest of the way to the Barclay bank. All totaled my business took me less time than I had anticipated. If I left within the hour I could be home in time for breakfast.

I slept most of the way as the carriage rocked rhythmically

along the road. I awoke to the warmth and sunlight through my carriage. The gates of Hedgewick Manor approached through the morning mist. My stomach growled as we rounded the gate in front of my home. As I got out and walked up the steps I could smell the starting of breakfast. I greeted Mrs. Potter at the front door and informed her I was famished. I went to my room to freshen up and then to the kitchen. Formal dining halls, I felt, were just that.....formal. Mrs. Potter was use to my presence at the staff table to eat. Scrambled eggs and toast were placed before me as I eagerly unfolded my napkin and began to devour breakfast. Several minutes later Rebecca eagerly entered the kitchen standing impatiently beside me. *"I thought I heard your carriage. Come! I have something to show you."* I finished the last bit of my toast and swallowed as I spoke. *"If it is proof of my madness I think I shall pass."* She smiled impatiently while I frowned and finished my juice. *"Actually....quite the opposite....please."* I reluctantly removed myself from the table and followed her into the library continuing my protests as we went. As I entered the room my library had been transformed into a whirlwind of newspapers strewn about with bits of paper attached to every lampshade, desk, drapery and mantle with straight pins. She watched me as she read my reaction to the chaotic room. Words scribbled with dates and phrases were on several of the torn scraps of paper attached to the lampshade in front of me. *"Please forgive the mess. It was necessary to decipher your incredible mystery."* I looked around still perplexed. *"I'm afraid you have me at a disadvantage."* She motioned for me to sit. I watched as she went through several old stacks of newspapers. *"You are truly amazing! No one would believe it. I've never documented such events......I......"* She looked up at me in her excited state and chuckled as she saw my look of concern. *"I know.....you think you have opened your house to a mad woman but there is a method to my apparent madness. You see..... your nightmares seem to be windows into the future."* Once again she could see the look of confusion on my face as I looked about the room. *"Look"* she said as she hurried about the room collecting certain bits of paper. She grabbed a newspaper, my diary and her notes and knelt down on the floor beside my chair. Her golden hair glistened from the flickering light of the surrounding lamps. The glow of the fireplace and crackling of wood added to the comforting feeling that ran through my body whenever this woman seemed to be near. I tried to focus on what she was eager to show me. I reached for my glasses that I sheepishly put on. *"Your hellish account of the coach accident on Waverly road last week was an actual event reported in the London Times two days later and here......"* She leaned over my lap to turn the pages of my diary back even further to last month. *"Your attention to detail was quite refreshing. It made my task much easier. Where is it? Ah.... here....the young boy who drowned in your dream was reported in the Times four days later..*" It was beginning to make sense to me. I was now seeing the path of her notes. I reached down to pick up a scrap of paper that had drifted down onto the floor. I accidentally brushed her hair with my cheek. The slight scent of roses on her hair once again caught me off guard as I closed my eyes and lingered a bit longer next to her softly scented hair. I sensed her turn and shot back to an upright position nearly dumping everything that was on my lap. Luckily she assumed my reaction was that of surprised discovery as opposed to impropriety. *"I hope I wasn't being too forward. I read your diary. Oh!.....But I didn't know what it was at the time. I'm sorry.....I"* I gathered the items on my lap, stood up and placed them on my desk. Clearly some proper space was needed on my part. I cleared a pathway and sat in the chair at my desk. Reading the pages of my diary I tried to distance myself from their memories. As I read her notes and read the marked pages of the various newspapers strewn about the desk I could see that her method of backtracking was taking shape. Rebecca got up and poured herself a glass of water. I watched as her lips caressed the rim of the glass. I looked back down at the newspaper article. I peered up from my glasses once more and noticed what toll this research had exacted from her. *"You haven't eaten anything in days.....have you?"* She coyly nodded and shrugged her shoulders. *"Shall I send Mrs. Potter in with some tea and sandwiches?"* She looked about the room and then looked at her reflection in the mirror. *"Oh dear! I do look a fright don't I?"* I took my glasses off, looked at her and smiled. *"I'm more concerned with your health than with your appearance."* She sat the glass down and walked over to me. *"So you don't care that I look like something the cats dragged in?"* Her teasing amused me as I chewed on the post of my glasses and leaned back in my chair. *"It has been my experience that cats don't generally bring in something that is alive so you see.....that merely proves my point! You desperately need some warm breakfast in that shell of a body your bent on abusing."* I rang for Mrs. Potter and starred at Rebecca until she listed her breakfast order. Once given, I had Mrs. Potter run a warm bath and escort a protesting Rebecca upstairs. Now that she was out of sight I could concentrate on her findings. It seemed that my nightmares had been strangely validated as entry after entry was noted in the various local newspapers. I sat back in my chair and looked about the disheveled room in silent lucidity. Not wishing to add to Mrs. Potter's frustration I decided to pick up bits and pieces of papers and tidy the stacks of newspapers that were strewn about the room. Rebecca's theories intrigued me as I viewed paper after paper of scribbled notes. I could see why she was an archeologist. Her methods of research and her tenacity made for an excellent researcher. I wasn't quite sure how this was to end my madness or even if it would, but having another person who knew of my plight was somehow comforting to me. As I picked up the notes I felt the presence of someone or something in the room. I looked around but saw no one. I was in need of some fresh air and sunlight.

The morning breeze was cool as it swept across the old stone patio. Like a breath of fresh air bringing with it the sweet scent of blossoming Jasmine. The garden released its scented treasures along with a palette of color. I watched as Robins gathered bits of twigs for their nest in the old oak tree outside the garden. *"Spring must be in the air."* Rebecca's voice was like that of a gentle wind. As I turned, her appearance caught me by surprise. For there before me stood a most beautiful vision. Her long golden brown hair shone like golden flax in the sunlight whilst her fine French tailored blouse, billowing in the breeze, tapered down towards her narrow waist. This was not a common sight for this day and age however, it was most pleasing to my eyes. Her trousers were a cream soft color like that of the roses that grew about the garden. Her riding boots were polished but had evidence of wear. I was at a loss for words. I quickly regained my composure thanks to Mrs. Potter and her mug of hot tea that she placed in front of me. *"Yes...a...spring....such a wondrous time for my garden and its inhabitants."* She draped herself across the stone wall as she gazed out into the garden. *"So.....what do you think?"* My confused look gave her cause to smile. *"You know...about my theory....what do you think?"* I sipped the warm tea and tried not to make direct eye contact. *"Well....your theory is interesting and certainly merits further research." "Excellent! When shall we start?"* I didn't realize how excited she would get at the prospect of researching my mystery. *"I though you needed to start your own research and excavation at Westmore?"* Rebecca sprung from the wall like a cat, planting herself beside me. *"I have already started my research thanks to your wonderful library. As for the excavation, I am to wait till my assistants arrive from the university. About 4 days."* I watched as she sipped some tea from my cup. *"I'm afraid I…a…have to take care of some business for my brother….a….in town. I will be gone most of the day. But I shall join you for….a… dinner…this evening. Perhaps we can continue with your theories then."* Never again do I ever wish to cause such sadness as I saw come over that beautiful face. Her smile faded and her head bowed. Alas, I could not resist such emotion. *"Very well then….I shall go to town and send a telegram. After that….I am yours to do with what you will."* A brilliant smile once again returned to Rebecca's face. *"Mrs. Potter! Get my carriage please."*

Chapter 2

MY RIDE INTO TOWN WAS BRIEF AS I CONDUCTED MY business once again for E.B. Randhorne and increased my brother's popularity by once again being in the know regarding financial matters. As I headed back towards my carriage I caught a glimpse of a beautiful ivory silk shirt in a storefront window. As I stood in front of the window visions of Rebecca seemed to wrap around the shirt. I walked in and did the usual 'purchasing a shirt for my brother' and had it wrapped with a golden bow. I was in no mood to argue or make a point. I wished only to return to my dear professor. As I peered out the window of the carriage I was almost glad to see the hustle of the city end and the tree lined forest begin. I sat back and tried to collect my thoughts of the past days. I had been attracted to women before but never sought to act upon it. Was I simply being teased by Rebecca or was she truly interested in me? As the carriage rocked to and fro additional horses hooves could be heard galloping alongside. After several shouts and a pistol being fired my carriage came to a halt. Highwaymen were still prowling the London roads at night but it was most unusual for them to be out during the day. I readied my pistol that my brother so fondly gave me and waited till my carriage door was opened. The black masked thief seemed to smile as he aimed his weapon into my carriage. *"My dear lady, I am afraid I must relieve you of your valuables."* Whilst charm and breeding go a long way, highway robbery does not sit well with me. *"My dear sir I fear You have picked a most unfortunate host for I carry no valuables on my person."* He continued to aim his weapon at me as he yelled at the driver to keep the horses still. *"My dear lady.....I must ask you to remove yourself from thy carriage.....NOW!"* As I exited I noticed he was alone. As he dismounted I raised my small pistol and fired one shot to his chest. As he doubled over in pain his fingers squeezed the trigger of his pistol. A shot rang out and caused his horse to rear up flailing its hooves up in the air and coming back down grazing my forehead. My driver helped me back up into the carriage as I ordered him to head for Waverly. My head was feeling warm and part of my hair seemed to be wet. My gloves were stained with blood as I gently felt my wound. A throbbing pain was inching its way forward as the carriage raced down the pathway of my home. I could no longer hold my head up and proceeded to curl up on the seat and wished the pain would end. I'm not sure when I came to but I felt as though I was falling. I awakened to a room full of concerned faces including Rebecca's. Mrs. Potter cleared the room except for Rebecca and old Dr. Graves. He bandaged my wound and left several packets of powder on my nightstand next to my diary and pen. As I gazed at Rebecca I drifted off to sleep. Days passed as beams of sunlight found there way past the drawn curtains. Eyes opened briefly if only to check the sunlight then close again to evening shadows. At one point I could even hear my brothers agitated voice as I was given a glass of water. But all seemed to blur as I slept.

Eleanor bolted upright as she wiped the sweat from her forehead. The grotesque visions played over and over in her mind forever etching the frightening images that plagued her sleep. Once again she reached for paper and pen to make note of this latest event. She wrote with chilling accuracy every detail of her disturbing visions. She noticed that at the end of her final sentence light was beginning to peer through her window. She looked at the clock on the dresser as its chimes rang out six times. Her bedroom door opened slowly. *"Lady Heddington? Are you alright?"* A concerned whisper and a familiar voice gave me cause to smile. *"Other than a rather large giant driving a carriage across my eyelids I'm fine….and please….."*

call me Eleanor." As she came into the light of the gas lamp her face was as I remembered......beautiful. She sat down beside me on the edge of the bed. I felt as though I were in a dream once more but her soft hand against my skin kept me in the reality of the moment. *"Oh Eleanor....Please don't frighten me like that again. My poor heart won't take it."* Her touch was so soft and gentle, her voice so soothing. *"I'll try not to. I would never do anything to endanger your precious heart."* Good lord! Why did I say that? Not only was my body in a weakened state but my mind was there as well. I looked into her eyes for an indication of impropriety but saw only tears. *"And why does my lady weep? I shall be on my feet tomorrow and we can pick up where we left off......going through your notes. Hush now...."* I could not control my reactions. I reached up and felt her silky hair that was now down about her shoulders, so inviting to the touch. She leaned forward, smiling as her eyes made contact with mine. I was thinking how soft her skin was as I propped myself up on a large feathered pillow. I needed a distraction before my injury would no longer excuse my actions. *"Why don't you bring your notes in here now and we can go over them."* Rebecca pulled back as if surprised by my request. *"What? Are you sure? Perhaps sleep...."* *"My nightmares need a distraction."* She paused for a moment and realized what I said was true. *"Ahhh....okay"* She stood up and straightened her shirt as if trying to regain her composure. She walked out as quietly as she had walked in. I laid back down to the comfort of my now warm pillow. My head was beginning to throb again so I took one of the doctors powders and mixed it with a glass of water that was on my nightstand. As gritty as it tasted, its slight mint flavor was rather pleasing. I laid back down and closed my eyes while I waited for Rebecca.

A flash of light, a roar of the surf and there I was standing on the edge of a cliff. As I looked over my shoulder I saw a young woman. She seemed to be arguing with an older man. As their argument grew in intensity the closer they moved towards the cliffs edge. My legs would not move. I try to speak but nothing comes out. He moves her to the edge as he places his hands around her neck. She cries out but I can do nothing. Finally, he pushes her, she looses her balance and in a flash of light she plummets to her death. I watch him move to the edge but still I cannot move. *"Lady Heddington......Eleanor....it's okay....open your eyes. Eleanor....."* Her voice, slowly pulling me, pulling me away from the cliff. *"Eleanor! Please....."* Rebecca's hands were pulling my shoulders towards her. *"I'm okay...Rebecca...I'm back."* She gathered the blankets around me. *"Your skin.....it's so cold. You need to get warm. Get under the covers. I can..."* *"It's alright Rebecca...really."* I held her now trembling hands and placed them over my heart. It seemed to have a calming effect on her. *"Can you tell me? You know....your vision?"* I gently placed my fingers over her lips. *"You brought me back this time and for that I thank you. You see....that is what is truly terrifying in my visions. I experience what the victims feel.It is as though I am part of them. But this vision...."* I hesitated to continue. *"Yes? What about this vision?" "I'm sorry....I never realized I could be helped. I'm glad you were here. I'm just so sorry It's been so.... different from what you envisioned." "Oh! And how exactly did I envision my visit here?"* Her eyes were playful yet inviting and her smile gently teasing. I reached over and kissed her, gently at first, then passionately as she returned my embrace. Realizing what I was doing I pulled back, waiting for the slap across my face. But to my surprise it did not come. Instead, my lips were greeted with a soft, gentle pleasure I had only dreamt about. I felt myself holding my breath, as if breathing would cause this moment to end. I reached out to touch her and was met with warmth that covered every fiber of my being. I wished for this moment to never end. If I was dreaming then surely I would wish never to awake. *"My dearest Eleanor....how is this possible?"* her whisper was like the wind. I felt it against my neck as she kissed me. *"How is it possible that you feel for me as I feel for you? Surely we will be struck down where we lay?"* I continued my passion as she nestled in beside me. *"My dear Rebecca.....unless you are expecting a visit from the English Ladies Society I think, at this moment, you have nothing to fear."* Her fingers began to explore my body. Wherever my skin lay exposed her touch caused it to flood with desire. What I wanted, what I dreamt of was not commonplace with a woman. Yet I desired it with every pulse of my rapidly beating heart. "***Perhaps you would be more comfortable under the covers?***" I said to her as I slid my hand down to caress the smoothness of her hips. She continued to kiss me as she moved to the other side of my bed. I turned away briefly to lower the lamp and remove my nightshift. It was then that I felt the warmth of her body next to mine. Hands that once were slow and gentle were now passionate and exploring. Never before had I been so taken with the touch and feel of another woman. The sensation of skin on skin caused my head to spin. "***Eleanor...are you alright?***" "***Yes my love...I was simply wishing for this moment to never end.***" Our fever was building as we moved on top of one another. "***Oh Rebecca....***" "***Oh....Eleanor***" Screams of delight were echoed into pillows as our desires reached their pinnacle. The perspiration on my body caused it to glisten in the lamp glow. The cooling breeze from the window drifted across my moisture laden body as I held Rebecca firmly against my bare breast. Rest came for both of us as we drifted off to a sleep we had never known before tonight. No nightmares, no dreamscapes, just peaceful, contented sleep.

As the morning light peered through my bedroom curtains I smiled as I thought of my wondrous dream. I stretched and yawned contented in the love and warmth that my dream had provided me. As I turned suddenly my pleasant dream turned into a frightful nightmare. For there beside me beautifully outlined in the sheets was Rebecca, sleeping soundly, peacefully and with a contented smile. What had I done? How could this impropriety have occurred? I went round and round in my mind yesterdays events that led to last nights indiscretion. All I could find was desire. The same shear desire that grew when I first met Rebecca in that hotel lobby. Had I possibly led her to commit this act? Will she awake and have several harsh words with me or even worse......refuse to speak to me? What would happen if word of this union leaked out to the Ladies Society or the Men's clubs of England? How would I handle my connection with E. B. Randhorne? My head was starting to reel and I remembered what events had put me in bed in the first place. I was suddenly interrupted by a soft hand reaching up to caress my shoulder. My body became rigid, hoping that no response would ward off further advances. But as my body became warm and desire roused within me I knew that my heart had been abducted and that all was lost. I turned to watch Rebecca awaken as I caressed her soft, supple skin. I kissed her cheek and moved down to her neck where my lips grew on fire and were driven by her arousing deep moans. She pulled my lips to hers and embraced my now quivering body. The clock chimed six times as I tried to pull away. *"Rebecca .....we must..."* The intensity of touch was unbearable. *"Yes.....yes...we must continue...from last evening."* I am still not sure how I did it but I managed to back up and off my bed. *"No! We must stop this....I.."* I desperately searched for the words but my pulse was racing and my lips were left wanting. As she reached out to touch me I grabbed her hands firmly and placed them at her side. *"Rebecca....please! We must be careful. My staff has their routine and one of which is to knock on my door and enter with morning tea. I cannot have you here in my bed....in my room, at least without changing some routines first. Surely you understand this?"* The look of annoyance was clear as she gazed out the window, sighed and put her gown back on. She walked back into her room via the shared door without a word spoken. I got dressed and awaited the familiar routine. Several minutes later Mrs. Potter knocked and entered with tea and muffins. *"Mrs. Potter....will you please ask Professor Almonte if she would like to join me on the terrace?"* She nodded and headed to Rebecca's door. I was surprised to see Rebecca already dressed. She entered my room, closed the door and starred at me. *"Rebecca... please try to understand I...."* She raised her hand, sighed and sat down beside me. *"I'm sorry...I have a nasty habit of being too pig headed at times. Rome wasn't built in a day and I seem to forget that periodically."* She leaned over and placed a gentle kiss upon my lips. *"I must return to the Ruins at Westmore and lay a foundation before my assistants arrive. I'm a little behind on my documentation so this will provide an excellent opportunity for me to get caught up."* My abruptness had definitely affected her. I felt as though she were running away. I couldn't loose her, not now. *"Rebecca… my love….please don't go away, not like this. I know you have work you must do. Far be it from me to distract you but….I love you….and I am in love with you. I have never had anyone of such importance in my life. I would redirect my life for you in a heartbeat….but you must understand what is at risk."* She stood up and walked to the window to look out. *"I know what is at risk, your lifestyle, your income, your precious E.B. Randhorne. I'm sure he would disapprove and probably fire you and there would go your income and status."* I did not know whether to smile or shake her. How could she be so attractive yet so infuriating at the same time? My anger was starting to show. I grabbed her by the arm and sat her on the edge of the bed. *"E.B. Randhorne would not disapprove nor would he fire me." "You can't be so sure of that." "Yes….I can be assured of it."* She looked at me with great interest. *"How? You have some sort of blackmail information on Mr. E.B. Randhorne?" "In a way….yes."* Her curiosity was peaked for she followed me as soon as I stood up and walked about the room. When I turned and nearly ran into her I leaned over, hugged her and whispered softly into her ear. *"I am E.B. Randhorne….. Eleanor Barton Randhorne Heddington at your service."* The quiet was almost deafening. It was as if I had knocked the wind out of her sails. Her demeanor softened and when she looked at me she smiled and then began to laugh. *"I'm so terribly sorry.....I had no idea that....."* *"Rebecca......I am serious."* I removed a letter from my desk that I had written to my brother. I then showed her a copy of a document signed by E.B. Randhorne. The signatures were clearly the same. She was visibly shaken. She felt for a chair and sat down slowly dropping the papers I had given her. I could see her mind going over the events that day in the hotel as I got dressed. She looked up at me once more. I smiled politely and sat across from her. *"I had no idea. I ...how did you....where does..."* Her sentences were fragmented as were her thoughts. She was clearly overwhelmed at this discovery. She, more than anyone, started to see the scope of my illusion. *"But Mr. Randhorne has been around for at least 15 years!"* I smiled as I looked around the room trying to choose my response carefully. *"Actually its more like 20 years."* *"But that can't be. Your only in your 30's."* I bent over a kissed Rebecca on the cheek then smiled at her as I spoke. *"Thank you my sweet....I don't wish to destroy your illusion but I'm 45 this October. Eleanor transformed into E.B. shortly after my brother moved here in 1887. Forgive me for springing this upon you. You touched a sensitive area and I foolishly responded in anger. Please forgive me? It was not my intention to confuse nor frighten you. I have worked very long and hard at this positioning of E. B. Randhorne. If I am to live amongst this society and abide but its rules and superstitions then I must learn to use them in my favor...don't you agree?"* I watched her nod as she continued to watch me. *"If I need a man to take care of my affairs then it should be one I can handle and agree with. Who better than myself."* I watched as she gazed out the balcony window. *"My dear brother was younger than me yet he was in control of our inheritance. His business deals were always questionable and I knew he would deplete our money within a few years. I got angry and devised a plan which I set in motion with the help of some of the more questionable characters down by the wharf. In return for their assistance the wharf received certain proceeds and new businesses were born as well as legitimate income for some. Once E.B. Randhorne was established I needed no one's assistance and took total control of all my brother's affairs. Quite a coup don't you think? "* I realized my sensitivity was getting the better of me so I quietly walked out towards the stairs. I grabbed the handrails and stopped, gazing down the stairs to the great hall. Perhaps I should have said nothing but I wanted her to know. I continued down the stairs and out the front door.

Rebecca stood motionless as she watched Eleanor leave. *"My dearest Eleanor....why do I constantly make you angry?"* I spoke softly as I watched my host walk down the stairs. I wanted to make up for my antagonistic behavior but I was confused. I could only imagine what it took for her to create the existence of E.B. Randhorne, not to mention the great personal risk in continuing the upkeep and monetary success. In the few days that I've known her she has shown me nothing but compassion, patience and understanding. The passion we shared….so intense….I've never been so….in love. She sets my mind and heart on fire. I must swallow my pig-headedness and talk to her. *"Excuse me miss but this letter came by post this morning."* Mrs. Potter handed me an envelope with the university seal on it. As I read it aloud my head began to ache. *"My research is overdue and my assistants are scheduled to arrive tomorrow. I haven't even mapped out the areas to be surveyed yet. These last few days must have been a dream."* Rebecca was drawn to the balcony as she saw Eleanor ride off towards the hills. *"Dear Eleanor…..I hope I haven't lost you. The intimacy we shared couldn't have been a dream."* She whispered to herself as she searched for some paper and pen.

My dear Eleanor,

I wish to apologize for any impropriety that took place during my stay. I fear I have made a terrible mess of things. Please forgive me for it was not my intention to upset or anger you. I must continue on with my work at Westmore and must leave for the ruins today. Thank you for your kind hospitality, lovely companionship and wonderful library. I look forward to seeing you again. Thank you again.

Yours Truly,

Rebecca

I summoned Mrs. Potter for a carriage and packed my things. As I sat in the carriage and gazed back at Hedgewick Manor I wondered if Eleanor would ever forgive me. She had an inner spirit that Rebecca had only read about in works by Shelly. Yet she realized that Eleanor had worked hard to get where she was and had to have suffered greatly in order to be so protective. Seeing the futility of her thoughts she took her notes and started back to work.

Eleanor rode back towards the stables as dusk approached. Mrs. Potter handed her Rebecca's note as she entered the hallway. Her heart sank and her eyes welled with tears as she read the note. An overwhelming sense of emptiness came over Eleanor as she walked to the library clutching the note. She sank into a chair and let the note drop to the floor. Her eyes were now clouded with tears. She hadn't meant to be so harsh regarding E.B. Randhorne. She knew that her sensitivity sometimes got the better of her. Eleanor stood up and walked out through the French doors to her garden. She looked back towards the house. The green vines she had tended to grew over the stone of the old Victorian manor so that the coldness that once existed now vanished. But the inside of the manor was still lonely and cold. Rebecca brought warmth into the manor and an enlightened passion to its owner. ***"It is I who have made a mess of things. I am the one who must beg for forgiveness for the impropriety*** *that took place."* The young birds twittered and cocked their head as she spoke to them. As they flew away she realized what she must do. *"Mrs. Potter! I need a carriage ! I must get to Westmore by morning."*

CHAPTER 3

R EBECCA STEPPED DOWN FROM THE CARRIAGE AS THE LAST
of the tents were erected. She was glad that several students
had arrived early. The local priest was talking to several townspeople
as Rebecca stepped up to greet him. *"Father Timmons?"* He turned,
smiled and spoke in a fine Welsh accent. *"Professor Almonte!
What a pleasure to see you again. I've taken the liberty of sending
your things to Mrs. Murphy's Inn down the road. Clean rooms,
good food and pleasant conversation or so she assures me."* She
thought him rather young to be running the local parish but the
people seemed to like him and therefore his services were usually
standing room only. She made her way past the gathering crowd to
a tent with a hand drawn sign that said **Mapping**. Within the tent

were several tables lined with the maps she had been studying for the past several days. She reached into her skirt pocket and pulled out her small notebook with her practically undecipherable notes. She smiled as she saw the notes she had made regarding Eleanor's dreams. She thumbed past them and took out a pencil and began to measure out a quadrant for the beginning of the dig. *"Excuse me....what's your name?"* She got the attention of a young female student who was writing her name on a check in list. *"Courtney Adams professor."* *"Well Courtney...I hope you had a pleasant trip down here."* *"Yes professor. I arrived with several freshmen this morning."* *"Do me a favor and round up everyone and tell them I'll be holding a meeting in a half an hour outside this tent."* With some organization starting to form Rebecca went back to her notebook. Months of deciphering historical accounts of events and cross referencing townships and historical markers had led her to this area of Westmore. She received permission from the Vicar to excavate a small parcel of land to the north that was owned by the church. His parish in return received a sizable donation from the university. It took Rebecca very little time to become immersed in her work. After her meeting with her assistants and volunteers she went back to her tent to continue her work for tomorrow. As dusk set in she found she could not control her feelings of sadness and emptiness regarding her dear friend Eleanor. She missed their conversations in the library and how nervous Eleanor would get around her but most of all she missed Eleanor's passion. It was something she had dreamt of but never had the opportunity to sample until Eleanor. The touch of another woman, the scent of another woman, the taste of another woman were all late night visions she hoped she would one day be able to feel. She suddenly realized why Eleanor was nervous that morning following their night of passion. *"I bet you it was her first time as well." "I think it's a first time for a lot of us."* Rebecca, not realizing she had spoken out loud, turned to see one of her older assistants standing by the flap of the tent. *"We've marked the areas you showed us on the map so we will be ready to start tomorrow. Some of us have settled in to our tents and were going to get something to eat. Would you like to join us?"* Rebecca starred down at her notes and stifled a yawn. *"Thanks for the offer but I think I'm going to go to my room at the inn and get a good nights sleep. See` you at six."* As much as Rebecca thought a bit of a distraction would have been helpful she did have a lot of work to catch up on. She would get up at her usual time of five o'clock and get an early jump on things.

The next day began in a flurry of students, shovels, and buckets. Everyone had first day excitement energy, as Rebecca like to refer to it. At around noon the young woman that had invited her out to dinner the other day entered the tent with a handful of penciled drawings. *"The top layer of soil has been removed and the first group has uncovered some sort of stone wall."* She rolled up several maps and carried them with her as she followed the young woman to the site of the discovery. As the day wore on the site slowly cleared of workers. Some remained in tents and some went to town. Rebecca sat down at a small makeshift desk outside the mapping tent and continued her notes. The weather was a bit chilly in the shade but wonderfully warm in the sun. She finally had finished the reports to the university and felt a small weight being lifted from her shoulders. But she then looked at the amount of work that had been done on the site and wondered if she would be able to complete the excavation project and publish her findings before her deadline. She was distracted as she watched a familiar carriage pull up beside the church. Rebecca stood up anticipating a familiar figure but as the carriage door opened she watched as a woman dressed in a long cream colored skirt and maroon colored blouse stepped down. The woman's hair was done in a French braid as one gloved hand reached up to check its position. It was Eleanor's coach but Eleanor's attire was always one of trousers, boots and long raven hair draped about lightly colored short sleeved shirts. Clearly this woman was not Eleanor but perhaps she was one of Eleanor's friends. She watched as the woman entered the church. She sat back down and continued her notes.

The days passed without incident until the fifth day when a small tunnel like structure had been revealed next to the rock wall. Inside the tunnel structure were pieces of pottery, jewelry and weapons dating back to the Celtic history of the region or as they were known in this area, Britanni. Each of the pieces were drawn where they were found, given numbers, logged in and tagged for shipment back to the university. By the second week the student assistants had their routines in place and were making headway in the excavation at Westmore. By the end of the third week the site began to take shape and clear views of walls and rooms were coming into view. No skeletons had yet been found but the pottery and jewelry were in almost every room of the unearthed area. Rebecca had finished cataloging the last jewelry discovery when she came across a note she had written for Eleanor. She reflected back and realized that she had not heard anything from her. She looked around as if she expected to see her. Two more weeks passed and the weather gradually began to change. The rains caused difficulty for everyone as the tents leaked, artifacts washed away and notes became blurry and smudged. Her students were reluctant to dive into mud and certain areas were inaccessible with heavy rain. She prayed for relief in the form of sun. All that was needed was a few days of sun to dry out tents, artifacts and researchers. Rebecca sat outside to write more notes in the damp air when she noticed a glimmer of sun trying to make its way through the clouds. It was cloudy but it was also the first day that rain was not falling even the clouds were not as dark and dismal as they had been. Her stomach growled as she took out her typewriter and placed it on the table. One of her young student assistants, Courtney Adams, brought Rebecca some food that was being prepared in the center of the camp. *"It's not exactly Paris cuisine but it is tasty."* The woman said as she placed a tray down on the table and walked back to her own tent. Rebecca thanked the woman and unfolded the napkin which held her silverware. She pushed and prodded the meat and carrots as if she were checking for signs of life. She decided upon a gravy laden potato as she impaled it with her fork. *"I don't think it will bite back but then again.....one never knows!"* That deep, sultry English voice was pleasantly familiar. Rebecca looked up and smiled. *"Eleanor !"* Rebecca shot up practically spilling her meal. The woman that stood before her did not resemble the Eleanor she remembered. Her hair was braided and pinned in a French curl, she was wearing a long tweed skirt along with a white Victorian high collar blouse and matching full length gloves. These subtle changes made Eleanor appear totally different. *"To what do I owe this sweet pleasure? Where have you been? I've missed you so....I..."* Rebecca noticed others looking and realized she was rambling so she smiled and sat back down in her chair and waited for Eleanor to speak. Eleanor breathed a sigh of relief at Rebecca's pleasant voice. It was if the past months issues were forgotten. *"I had to straighten out some things with our dear Mr. Randhorne. I also wish to offer an apology from Mr. Randhorne and his secretary."* Eleanor moved back slightly wishing to keep a safe, respectable distance from Rebecca as she spoke. *"Mr. Randhorne apologizes for the excessive trips that he's requested from his secretary. As for his dedicated, extremely loyal secretary....well.....she apologizes for being angry and quite foolish regarding her guest. She misses you and hopes that her relationship with you can be mended."* Eleanor sat down and placed a single red rose next to Rebecca as she awaited her response. Rebecca looked into Eleanor's eyes as she continued to smile. *"It is I who needs to apologize to the secretary. I think I was somewhat jealous of her relationship with E.B. Randhorne, silly really. My relationship with the secretary was never really broken so mending it shouldn't be an issue.* Rebecca's gaze was piercing as she smiled slyly back at Eleanor. *"I definitely miss your hair down about your shoulders."* Rebecca said as she took in the image of Eleanor standing before her. Rebecca could no longer continue the charade. She stood up and leaned in across the table as close to Eleanor as it would allow. *"Forgive me for being so forward but....I miss not being able to touch you."* Eleanor bowed her head in embarrassment for she could feel her face flush with red. She removed a small piece of paper from inside her gloved hand. *"I've been doing some research of my own and have reserved two adjoining rooms at the inn at the end of town. I would be most delighted if you could join me this evening for dinner."* Eleanor's radiant smile, coupled with her smooth deep voice, were hypnotic to Rebecca. *"I would be honored." "Wonderful ! Your room is available anytime. Shall we say around 6:00?" "I look forward to it."* Both women stood for a moment looking at one another as if they had been apart for years. Rebecca knew what she was about to do was chancy but she was relying on Eleanor's sense of propriety to control her. She stepped around the table and gave a friendly hug to Eleanor. Eleanor moved back slightly startled yet keeping some space between the two. She then hugged Rebecca back, turned and headed for her carriage. Rebecca closed her eyes as her body began to melt. She had missed Eleanor so and was afraid that their night of passionate impropriety had forever changed their relationship. She was glad for once that she was wrong. She closed her eyes and remembered Eleanor's touch, her breath, her voice. Was she being foolish, hopelessly romantic perhaps? Here she was at 32 years of age with several major accomplishments for a woman and yet love and romance had eluded her. The men she had known were nice and respectable but were always lacking within Rebecca's standards. She was an intelligent woman with certain hopes of a career instead of marriage. That alone had made her a pariah in some circles. She opened her eyes once again and smelled the crisp, cold air. She looked down at her plate and then caught sight of one of the local scavenging dogs. She placed the metal plate with her food down on the ground for the hungry dog. She chuckled as she realized that the Celts probably fed their hunting dogs the same way within their castles. She sighed, looked around at the dwindling staff and went on to her tent to pack.

Chapter 4

THE PUB WAS ITS USUAL MIX OF LOCALS AND VISITORS AS Eleanor asked for a corner table near a large picture window. It was as private as she could see within the inns configuration. She had so wanted to dress in her usual casual comfort of trousers, shirt and tie but did not wish to draw any unnecessary attention. She chose instead, a tasteful Victorian gown of dark green with flecks of gold woven in the fabric. Eleanor watched as the busy cobblestone street cleared. As the sun went down vendors locked up their barrows and headed for the local pub across the street. It looked as though it were a Toulouse Lautrec painting that had come alive with a flurry of color. Rebecca appeared from around a carriage as Eleanor watched her navigate through the streets activity. Eleanor's heart raced as she watched Rebecca. She wanted to order an American whiskey but as propriety demanded she ordered a glass of wine. Although this was not widely accepted she felt that here in this small town it would be an acceptable request from a tourist. As Rebecca entered she nodded as some fellow research students passed by. As she removed her cape she glanced around the room and saw Eleanor sitting at a corner table. Her smile broadened as she made her way to the table. *"Sorry I'm late. I....."* Eleanor stood and helped her off with her scarf. *"It's alright. I was reacquainting myself with this glass of wine."* Both women sat down and gazed at one another. They were interrupted by the old waiter who frowned as Rebecca ordered a hot toddy. The restaurant was crowded and Eleanor had to speak up slightly in order for Rebecca to hear her. *"So.....how is your research going?"* She watched as Rebecca seemed to settle in and relax as she spoke. *"Well....we've uncovered a stone wall and a tunnel like structure that housed various pottery and jewelry which seem to be Celtic in nature. I'm not really sure what the structure is yet since the weather has been so horrid the past couple of weeks. We almost lost several pieces in the mud! "* *"Weren't the Celts economy mainly pastoral and agricultural? I mean ...why would you find pottery and jewelry and nothing else? "* Rebecca grabbed a scone as she listened to Eleanor's question. *"I simply think we haven't made it to that room and level yet. If the wall represents a castle like structure then we should find weapons of some sort..... swords, spears, that sort of thing. They really had no urban life to speak of. Each of the tribes were led by a king and was further divided by class into the priests, warrior nobles, and commoners."* *"Where did the Druids come in?"* *"They were the priests. You see, the functions of priests, religious teachers, judges and civil administrators were performed by Druids. There were three known classes of Druids: prophets, bards and priests. And catch this....They were assisted by female prophets or sorcerers."* Rebecca stopped and watched Eleanor's eyes as they twinkled. As the waiter returned Rebecca's concentration was broken. *"I had no idea you were so well versed in the history. I should have known by your library. You did read every book in it didn't you."* Eleanor couldn't help but lean in towards Rebecca. *"Well... I had to occupy myself while E.B. was on his adventures so.....yes....I have read them....all."* They each ordered the fish speciality of the evening and continued talking. *"So...what else do you know about the Celtic people?"* Eleanor politely reached for a scone and buttered it on one side then placed it down as she spoke. *"I know that they were a people that dominated much of western and central Europe in the first millennium BC and that they gave their language and religion to other peoples of those areas.. I know that Celtic mythology includes Earth g-ds, various woodland spirits and sun deities; that Celtic art is considered the first great contribution to European art and although the art was influenced by Persian, Greek, Etruscan and Roman art that it developed distinct characteristics. How's that for a start?"* "*Truly remarkable, the woman has a brain too!*" As the evening wore on the restaurant began to clear to the point of slower service and the arrival of their dinners. Apologies were given by the waiter and an extra bottle of wine was left. Once alone again they began to laugh at their own behavior. *"I've missed you so. I thought you were horribly angry with me so I immersed my self in my work."* Eleanor sipped her wine as she listened to Rebecca. Her voice was alive with passion and feeling for her work. Eleanor realized that no matter how fulfilling her life seemed now she was missing something vital......true passion. Rebecca continued to fill in Eleanor on the digs recent discoveries and her war with the mud. Eleanor listened to her, content on smiling and watching her animated explanations. *"But listen to me....I'm rambling on like some giddy school girl. How have you been?"* Eleanor wanted to say 'better since she was here with her' but thought better of it. *"I'm fine. Mrs. Potter still worries when I stay away too long. She says after the carriage incident she would have thought I had learned my lesson. E.B. Randhorne now owns a full line of ships traveling to the Orient and the Americas. He's requested that his brother take a more active part since the more popular E.B. gets the more publicity he has to avoid."* "*Is he still afraid of exposure?*" Eleanor sipped her wine as she continued. *"Very much so. But E.B. isn't quite sure what to do about it."* Rebecca reached over and removed Eleanor's small, round lightly tinted glasses exposing familiar dark circles around Eleanor's eyes. *"I see we still suffer from nightmares."* Eleanor turned away slightly to avoid Rebecca's penetrating gaze. *"May I get you ladies some of our homemade desserts?"* Both women graciously declined and sat quietly gazing out the large picture window as they drank their tea. Eleanor broke the silence. *"They're not as frequent as they once were. I seem to be able to keep them at bay by......"* Eleanor leaned slightly and whispered. *"thinking of you."* Those words caused Rebecca to blush and then smile. *"I think it's time I excused myself. I've had a long day and need to get some well needed rest. Shall I see you at breakfast tomorrow?"* Eleanor smiled and continued to sip her tea. *"That would be wonderful. See you tomorrow."* Proper appearances had been made and now it was time to try and contain ones feelings of anticipation. Eleanor gazed out the window trying not to acknowledge the excitement that was beginning to well inside her. Finally, she looked at the clock on the wall, checked her father's pocket watch that she carried for luck and left money along with a tip on the table. Once upstairs she could hear no sounds emanating from the adjoining room. Was it possible that Rebecca was truly tired and went to bed? As Eleanor changed into her night shift a discreet knock was heard from the adjoining room. Eleanor raced to the door but unbolted it slowly. As the door opened their stood Rebecca in her pale blue robe. *"I thought you'd never get here!"* She grabbed Eleanor's hand as she walked through the door to the middle of the room. A quick glance around revealed that the doors were locked and the shades drawn. Eleanor closed her eyes as Rebecca's hands began to touch her cooled skin. The soft gentle touch of lips against skin created an intense desire that threw both women into intimate caresses, bodies entwined creating a heat like no other. As Eleanor reached up to remove Rebecca's robe she felt her body tremble. As the robe slowly slid off of her shoulders beautiful bare skin was exposed. Eleanor gently brushed the nape of Rebecca's neck with her lips. Stifled moans were trying to be controlled but as the intensity of the touch increased so did the lack of control. As the bodies fell into the thick downy sheets rain could be heard pelting the roof of the inn. Bodies began to glisten with sweat as they were highlighted by the flickering lamplight. The wanting that had been left by their parting was now filled with heat and desire. Where Eleanor's kisses were soft and gentle Rebecca's were rough and uncontrollable. Rebecca felt as though her heart would jump out of its shell at any moment. The intensity of their lovemaking stimulated every fiber of their bodies, the rain masking whispers of passion. As the night wore on their dalliance subsided and gave way to gentle sleep, each one caressing the other in loving embrace.

Eleanor could see the rain causing deep impressions in the mud. She could see Rebecca down within one of the tiny tunnels busily excavating an iron shard. She could only watch as the rain caused the dirt to change into rolling mud flowing into the tunnels at increasing speed. She then saw Rebecca scrambling to get out of the area as it rapidly filled with mud. But the more she moved the deeper the mud traveled. Suddenly Rebecca was engulfed in mud. Others tried to reach her but to no avail. The water was too deep and the mud was too thick. Rebecca was drowning before her eyes. Eleanor shot up in terror. Her sudden movement awakened Rebecca. She remembered that terrified look from before as she wiped her eyes trying to focus. **"Shhh.....It's okay, you're here with me. Eleanor?.....Eleanor......"** The tears began to flow from Eleanor as Rebecca held her sobbing body. There was a sudden emptiness Eleanor had never known before, an emptiness that sickened her beyond belief. She held her hands to her face trying to control the wave of sickening emotions that were surfacing. Rebecca felt for her robe beside the bed and located the large pocket from which she removed a silver flask. She handed it to Eleanor. **"Here....drink this."** The slightly caustic liquid warmed Eleanor as it slid down her throat. She took another shot of the amber colored liquid and began to catch her breath. Rebecca could feel Eleanor start to breathe normally. **"Now.....tell me....what did you dream?"** At first Eleanor refused to reveal the horrible vision. But Rebecca knew how to soothe and how to coax Eleanor. She sat quietly as Eleanor relived the vision. Afterwards, Rebecca held Eleanor and gently, lovingly relaxed her into sleep. She watched Eleanor as she slept. She knew that Eleanor's visions came true but did she have the power to stop them? Did she ever try to change the events or was she an unwilling victim to the hellish nightmares. She remembered that Eleanor had mentioned the last nightmare was different than the others but had successfully skirted relaying the events to her. Perhaps she needed to press the issue and find out what made that nightmare different. But she looked down at Eleanor who was peaceably sleeping in her arms. She would tackle the issue in the morning but for now she would hold the woman she loved tightly within her arms, protecting her from the world outside.

A messenger arrived early as Eleanor walked towards the front desk. She was going to check the papers mainly to get her mind off her hellish nightmare and to glance at what new cargo had arrived from the various shipping fleets she now owned. She successfully managed to sneak out without arousing the sleeping Rebecca. The young man at the front desk smiled as he walked towards Eleanor. *"Lady Heddington?"* He seemed to stand on his toes to get her attention. *"Yes?"* *"A telegram just arrived for you."* He handed her the telegram as she searched her purse for a farthing. After paying the young man for his trouble she walked towards a small table by a window and sat down. The telegram was from her brother. A government agent was looking for E.B. Randhorne to discuss several questionable business ventures. Her brothers use of the word 'please' several times within the telegram made her realize he was frightened. Eleanor was now torn between duty and protecting Rebecca. If her visions did become reality then Rebecca's life was in danger and Eleanor was not going to loose her that way. She knew the discovery of E.B. Randhorne would one day cross her path. She just never realized it would be so soon. *"Good Day Lady Heddington."* Eleanor turned around to see Rebecca's irritated face. *"Professor Almonte.....so nice to see you again."* Eleanor could tell she was upset at her absence this morning. *"I'm terribly sorry but I am late for a meeting and will have to take a rain check on that breakfast."* Eleanor was hoping to mend the problem so she folded up the note and placed it within her purse. *"Will you be working on the cavern you discovered the other day?"* Eleanor tried to act casual as she spoke but Rebecca saw through it. She pulled her quietly aside and whispered. *"It's okay. I'll heed the warning. Don't worry."* A young messenger popped his head around the corner as he called out for Professor Almonte. Both women turned in his direction. Rebecca waved and got his attention. *"Professor... your carriage awaits you."* She tipped him as she turned back towards Eleanor. *"I must go to my meeting since I was the one that called it...........Ride with me......please?"* As

Eleanor was about to agree another messenger appeared calling for Lady Heddington. Her brother had sent a carriage to take her to the train station where he would meet her to discuss their dilemma. *"I fear I cannot. I must meet with my brother. Just promise me you will not set foot in that cavern."* Rebecca breathed heavily. *"Please Rebecca!"* The urgency in her voice made Rebecca agree she also realized that her irritation was not really with Eleanor but with herself for being pig- headed again. Eleanor reached out and took Rebecca's hand. She gently held it within hers. *"I'll tell you what you want to know tomorrow....okay?"* Rebecca longed to kiss Eleanor to comfort her but the openness of the inn lobby dictated otherwise. *"I'll see you tomorrow."* Eleanor placed her glasses on as she watched Rebecca head for her carriage. She knew this day would be a long one as she walked to her own carriage.

Chapter 5

"**W**HERE IS SHE? SHE'S USUALLY VERY PROMPT." THE tall young man with dark hair and fair complexion paced back and forth as he watched for a familiar carriage. The shorter man standing off to the side with blonde hair reassured the man of her presence. *"I know everything will get settled. She will figure something out."* As the tall man turned, a familiar carriage pulled up at the station. The train station was always busy but on the platform the last of the passengers boarded the train heading back to London which left the platform deserted. The blond haired man jumped off the barrel he was sitting on when he saw Eleanor. *"Robert ! Peter! What are you doing here?"* She expected to see her brother Robert but not her childhood friend Peter. *"Someone* *had to keep your brother calm.*" Peter had been her neighbor whom she rode horses with as a child. When they grew up, Peter had asked for Eleanor's hand in marriage but Eleanor respectfully declined. From that time on Peter had been her confidante and truest friend. *"Well my dear little sister....I wonder what type of rabbit you'll pull out of your hat this time?"* He called for a carriage. *"Come! Lets go"* Eleanor halted and looked back at Peter. *"Robert...I cannot go with you. I have a rather pressing matter back at Westmore."* Both men were shocked. *"Are you mad? What could possibly be more pressing than this?"* Roberts slightly raised voice was drawing some attention. Peter pulled them both into an area void of passengers and prying ears. *"Look....I've thought about the situation and have booked passage for Mr. Randhorne on the next ship to the Americas. This agent will either have to wait until E.B. returns or he will have to deal with his most trusted secretary. Stop worrying."* She turned to Peter and placed a firm hand on his shoulder. *"And for G-d sakes Peter.... Stop looking like the world is coming to an end."* Eleanor kissed her brother and gave Peter a fond hug. *"E.B. Randhorne's solicitor will deal with this matter for now, Gentlemen"* She walked to the porter and asked where she could send a telegram. She walked over to the telegraph office as her astonished brother and friend looked on. Once several telegrams were sent Eleanor found the nearest carriage and headed back towards Rebecca's excavation site.

Meanwhile, Rebecca conducted her meeting without incident as the rain poured down on the slightly leaky tent. She only had two weeks left to make her report and conclude her findings at the site. When asked about the cavern she stated she was taking her time to check with other teams and that due to the muddy conditions would postpone the excavation of the sight until further notice. Several detailed artifacts had been cataloged and sent off to be displayed in the university's museum. As the meeting broke she went over several of her assistants notes. One in particular caught her eye. She looked in one of her many reference books for the design she was thinking the drawing resembled. The marking in the drawing she had seen just recently. She called to one of her assistants. *"Do you know if these sketches are Mary's?"* The young woman pointed to the three initials at the bottom of the drawing. *"Yes professor. These are Mary's. See....MCM Mary Clark Masterson."* *"Where is Mary?"* *"I don't know professor. I think she was finishing up her mapping of the cavern."* *"What? I thought I said that sight was off limits?"* The young woman looked perplexed. *"Well....you said due to the mud you were postponing the excavation of the site. I didn't hear you say it was off limits."* Rebecca stood up and put on her raincoat. *"Damn it!"* *"Professor? What's wrong?"* She grabbed a lit lantern as she spoke. *"That site is too damn dangerous in this weather, that's what."* She hurried out into the deluge.

At that moment Eleanor's head began to ache. Her chest tightened and she had difficulty breathing. She couldn't explain it but she could feel Rebecca. She hurried the carriage but knew that riding horseback would be quicker. She quickly changed into trousers, boots and a silk blouse. She grabbed her long coat from the top rack and stopped the carriage. She then had the driver unhitch the team of horses and replace the bridle on one. *"But miss....there's no saddle?" "It's alright. I don't have time for one. I'll send word for a replacement horse as soon as I get to town."* Eleanor rode off into the dense rain at full gallop.

The rain continued as Rebecca watched the puddles in front of her increase to small craters. She could see the dim glow of a lantern as she approached the tunnel. She stood out side and called for Mary Masterson. As the light grew brighter she could see the young student crawling up onto the muddy steps. Just as she propped up her lantern onto the entryway, a wash of muddy water raced down from the middle of the camp. The force of the mud knocked tents over and moved crates of equipment from secure locations to precarious ones. As the mud continued to flow it gained speed and bits of debris.

Eleanor doubled over in pain as she rode hard in the rain. *"No !"* She cried out as she saw her vision once again. She could barely see her hand in front of her face yet she continued on. She cursed the day her visions started and she wished she had stayed with

Rebecca. *"I will not let you die!"* She shouted as if the forces that be would hear her. She could see faint lights in the distance. Just a little bit further.

Rebecca turned and watched as the tents behind her became a mass of sticks and canvas. Suddenly, without warning the ground gave way beneath her feet and Rebecca went cascading down towards the tunnel. The same tunnel that according to Eleanor would be her tomb. She scratched and clawed her way through the mud but to no avail. As she reached the entry to the tunnel Mary grabbed hold of her to try and prevent her from being washed down into the tunnel. The mixture of mud and clay was too slippery and Rebecca was washed down the tunnel with the debris from the tents. *"No! Professor!!!!! Someone please….help me…..please. Can anyone hear me?"* The young student yelled and shouted but the force of the rain merely blended her frantic cries of help into the roar of the muddy water.

Eleanor reached the edge of the encampment and saw evidence of the mudslides destruction. Once she dismounted she could no longer see but it wasn't due to the rain. She saw her vision in front of her and nothing else. It was blurry and out of focus. Eleanor stumbled and trudged her way through the mud and onrushing chaos.

Several people braved the rain and mud to pull Mary from the wall she was clinging to. She was brought to one of the four remaining tents that were still standing. Meanwhile, the mud and debris finally wedged Rebecca against a wall that was slowly giving way at the back of the tunnel. As the mud slid down the rock Rebecca could see what had stopped her descent. There before her was a large stone cross with ornate engravings of earth gods and what looked like woodland spirits. She chuckled slightly as she realized that she would probably be buried with this great discovery. Her lantern was still upright and glowing so she reached up and placed it above her on a small ledge.

Eleanor fell into the mud puddle and crawled to a stone sitting upright in the mud. She tried to shout but only got a mouth full of water. A wood crate marked supplies floated towards her. She smashed open the crate with a nearby stone to find shovels and ropes mixed in with several lanterns. She grabbed the rope and used one of the shovels to dig into the ground as she crawled. The vision once again moved her forward. She could now feel that she was sliding downhill. She managed to tie one end of the rope to the stone that was sitting upright and the other end around her waist. She dug the shovel into the mud to try and hold her position but the debris and crates pushed her off balance. Her oil canvas coat acted like a slide and down she went in the direction of gravity. She had stopped, apparently hung up on something. *"Bloody Hell!"* she cried. *"Hello? Is …someone there?"* *"That's a matter of opinion. My body feels like its in pieces but I think I'm here."* That slight bit of sarcasm and deep sultry tone sounded familiar. *"Eleanor! Is that you?" "Rebecca! Are you alright?"* Both women began to laugh as they looked around at the volume of mud around them. Eleanor checked the rope around her waist to make sure it was still there. She then inched forward past several piles of wood and canvas debris. There before her covered in mud with brilliant glistening eyes was Rebecca. She crawled over to her, reached up and held her face. She then kissed her and held her vowing to never let go. *"I thought I had lost you. The rain and the mud.....I couldn't see anything. I though you promised to stay away from this accursed tunnel?" "Believe it or not I wasn't in the tunnel. I was outside calling one of my students out of it when the ground gave way and here I am."* Eleanor continued to hold her as she reached behind. *"Here my love......I brought you a shovel. You can't say I never brought you anything."* Eleanor's humor belied the grave danger they were in. The rain turned the clay and surrounding dirt to thick mud. And once flushed into the tunnel they were rapidly being entombed. The clay made it difficult to move and the debris was too large and bulky to clear. Suddenly Eleanor felt a tug on the rope around her waist. She pushed as much of the debris and mud from the way she came down. *"Hold on to me." "Alright but I can't move very much."* Eleanor looked up at the ceiling of the tunnel. She was happy for a small miracle. The tunnel was made of unusual primitive interlocking stone. The water didn't seem to be seeping from the ceiling which was good news. Eleanor figured it would hold. Another tug was felt and Eleanor held Rebecca as tightly as she could. Her coat once again served as a slide but this time she was sliding up as she and Rebecca were pulled towards the tunnel opening. Once at the top the rain had subsided slightly and a muted sound of cheers and shouts of 'professor' could be heard. Both women were unrecognizable as the mud dripped off their bodies. Several students had buckets of water and were attempting to wash off the women. Eleanor was a bit luckier than Rebecca in that once she removed her coat only a wet shirt and slightly muddy trousers and boots were seen. Amidst the flurry of students hands, buckets and discussion the two women gazed at one another in grateful silence. It was as though they were communicating on a higher level. *"Is everyone alright?" "Yes professor. Everyone is accounted for but I'm afraid the artifacts from this morning were washed away." "No matter.....as long as everyone is safe."* She gave several students the job of reclaiming what the mud and rain had taken. The rest of the students were given emergency vouchers for several of the inns that were in town. Those that already had rooms would double up with those who did not. Eleanor helped several rather portly girls with stacking the destroyed canvas tents and their poles for removal. Several hours later Rebecca gave the all clear and ushered everyone back to inns to clean up and rest. They would report back tomorrow morning at 9 a.m. ready to work. Eleanor checked her pocket watch: 3:00 Someone should have arrived by now with another horse to pick up the carriage she left. She looked around at the now deserted site. Rebecca started to sneeze and mud flew off of her totally caked hair. *"Well, I don't know about you but I definitely need a bath."* Eleanor held her sides and smiled. *"That sounds wonderful. But I think your room is the one with a tub."* *"Well then, we will just have to share..... won't we."* Eleanor wondered if the bath would make her bruised sides feel better. She would wait to tell Rebecca of her injury. *"I think we will have to wait for a carriage."* *"I can drop you off somewhere if you like."* Both women turned to see the muddy face of Mary Masterson. *"Are you sure you have room?"* *"No problem. I have one of those new Horseless Carriages. Come .....take a look."* As the woman uncovered the carriage Rebecca and Eleanor shook their heads in amazement. *"Come on...get in!"* The women did as they were told and had an enjoyable ride into town. They apologized for the flinging mud on the upholstery and laughed as they quickly raced up the stairs past the desk clerk before anyone could see them.

Chapter 6

"*M*r. Winthrop it is imperative that I speak *with Edward Barthalomew Randhorne. This is a very urgent matter!*" Peter swallowed nervously as he spoke. "*I understand that Mr. Doyle however, as I explained to you before his secretary Ms. Heddington has stated that he is on a ship to the Americas. It left yesterday and I really have no way of getting in touch with him. She handles all of his affairs so she is the one you really should be talking to regarding this matter.*" The short man with the mustache paced back and forth as his face flushed with irritation. "*Mr. Winthrop do you realize the gravity of this situation? Mr. Randhorne's fund can be seized and all accounts frozen. Not to mention the embarrassment to Mr. Randhorne* *and his clients."* Peter held his ground and said nothing. The little man sneered as he spoke. *"Fine ! Then where is this…. Ms. Heddington?"* Peter turned to his desk and looked for the paper with Eleanor's address on it. *"Here we are, Waverly Manor. Shall I call a carriage?"* The irritated man grabbed the paper and stormed out the door. *"Is he gone?"* Eleanor's brother Robert peered around the corner of the office. *"Yes, thank G-d but I'm not sure how long we can keep up this charade."* Robert walked to Peter's side. *"Don't worry. When Eleanor says she will take care of it…..well it gets taken care of. She obviously has something going on in Westmore so we will just have to wait."*

Meanwhile, in the south sea of England, on a moon lit night, the Jade Star moored and offloaded crew and their cargo of linseed oil and cotton onto an awaiting steamer. The captain and four other men remained on board as a man with a hooded cape, dressed in trousers and boots came aboard with a small trunk. *"Captain Connor….as agreed…. 100 gold sovereigns and proof of accounts in the Barclay bank set up for you and four of your men, a…. Therwood Feebs, John Mims, Alfred Warton and Billy Tubs. Please have your men sign here."* The hooded man removed his cape to reveal the face of a young woman. She smiled as she adjusted the collar around her neck. The young woman handed the captain the paper as his men stood behind her. As each of the men signed the paper she watched as the last crate was loaded onto the steamer. He handed her the signed paper while his men opened the trunk. *"I take it everything is in order?"* The captain nodded as his men gazed at the gold. The young woman placed the hood of her cape back on and headed back to the steamer. *"Alright you....'noblemen' let's do our part of the bargain."* They continued to sail south towards Spain. The hooded figure stood on the deck of the steamer and watched as the silhouette of the moon hid behind oncoming clouds and the Jade Star sailed out of sight.

Chapter 7

ELEANOR CAUTIOUSLY CLIMBED INTO THE WARM TUB OF soapy bubbles closing her eyes as her body melted into the water. She had already washed her face in the sink but it still felt as though it were caked with mud and clay. She opened her eyes as her body felt a disturbance in the water. Rebecca sat across from her as the bubbles floated around her neck. *"I may never get out. They'll have to carry my shriveled, pruned body away."* Eleanor started to unbraid her hair as Rebecca placed a hand on hers. *"Here.....let me help you with that."* Rebecca stood up with the soapy bubbles sliding down her beautifully curved body. She slid in behind Eleanor as Eleanor moved forward. Once her hair was unbraided Eleanor leaned her head back. Rebecca began to stroke her hair and wash it. Eleanor thought she had died and truly gone to heaven. Rebecca placed her arms around the relaxed woman and pulled her to her wet, warm body. Eleanor floated with both mind and body as she rested her head on Rebecca's shoulder. The women laid quietly, floating the bubbles around their tired bodies. Rebecca whispered as she broke the silence. *"You know...I never got to properly thank you for saving my life."* Eleanor adjusted turning her body slightly to the side. *"All in a days work m'lady."* Rebecca leaned over and kissed Eleanor gently on the lips. Eleanor responded reaching a soapy hand up to caress Rebecca's face. Her sides ached as she moved. *"You may not mind shriveling like a prune but I do. May I offer you my bed as a plausible substitute?"* The question did not need an answer. Both women stood up and reached for their towels which they wrapped around their wet bodies. Eleanor headed for the bed in her room as Rebecca pulled the plug on the tub. As Eleanor pulled back the covers she whinced as the pain around her waist surfaced. She removed the towel as Rebecca entered the room. *"Oh my G-d!"* She said in horror as she looked at the large black and blue bruise that had formed around Eleanor's waist. *"Oh come now.....surely my body does not displease you that much."* Eleanor tried to joke as Rebecca came closer to examine the injury. *"What have I done to you?"* Eleanor got into bed and pulled the covers around her. *"You my love have done nothing. Shut up and get into bed."*

Eleanor held the covers up as Rebecca slid in next to her. She gently touched the bruised area as tears welled up in her eyes. Eleanor looked up and saw Rebecca in tears. *"Hey….what did I tell you? This is not your fault. It's just a bruise. It will heal."* Rebecca swallowed as she tried to speak through the tears. *"Being around me….. will….. only cause you pain."* Eleanor kissed her on the cheek as she whispered to her. *"Nonsense! You're just upset and understandably so but …."* *"Don't you see….you were almost killed by that highwayman and now this!"* Eleanor could see that she would have to address this issue carefully. *"That is hardly a conspiracy and you're forgetting something crucial."* *"What's that?"* *"It is I who had the visions long before I met you and as if that wasn't enough proof, my adventures before you have caused….."* Eleanor sat up and started to point to different parts of her body. *"A broken finger, two cracked ribs and a knife wound. So you see….compared to before I met you ….well…..your much better for my health."* She turned, kissed Rebecca and leaned her against a soft pillow as she gently rubbed her shoulder. *"You and your mind need to relax. The truth of the matter is …..I love you and I would go to any lengths to keep you safe and in my arms."* Rebecca had never heard anyone say the things that this woman was saying. She had dreamed it but never thought it would happen to her. The woman she was next to had proved her love. Rebecca had only to accept it. She laid back and felt Eleanor's tender kisses on her shoulder. She reached up and held Eleanor's face in her hands. *"I've been so…foolish. I love you so much….I…I sometimes think you're a dream and if I believe in you too much you'll….. fade away."* "You don't have to worry. I have no intention of going anywhere for quite sometime." "What about that business with Randhorne?" "Sshhhh. It's being taken care of as we speak. Now relax and hand me that packet of white powder on the table beside you." Rebecca handed her the packet. Eleanor placed the powder in a small glass of water and stirred it with her finger. She drank half and gave the other half to Rebecca. *"Go on…..drink it."* She made a face as she sampled the bitter mixture. *"It's only aspirin and it will relieve the aches your body will develop after it recovers from your mud bath you took today."* "What in the world is as…aspirin?" Rebecca did as she was told and handed the glass back to Eleanor. *"It's an acid that is found in the bark of a willow tree. It was used by the Greeks and I'm told by my ship captains that some Native Americans use it. I just know it works."* She then folded the covers around her and pulled Eleanor to her. She began to kiss her shoulder as her fingers felt her hard nipples. The sounds of her pleasure moved Rebecca into a frenzied excitement. After awhile of intimate lovemaking their bodies feel into restful slumber each with their arms around each other.

CHAPTER 8

REBECCA WAS THE FIRST TO WAKE TO THE SOUNDS OF SONG birds outside her window. She tried to move the covers but realized that Eleanor had wrapped them around, entwining both women. As she lay there gazing at Eleanor her body began to awaken and as such the muscle pains began to surface. She then remembered Eleanor's bruise and gently pulled the covers from around them to look at her injury. With Eleanor still asleep Rebecca could take a closer look at her lover's injury. It seemed to have darkened since yesterday and looked quite terrible. She glanced over at the time: 6:00 am. She turned and kissed Eleanor gently on the lips as she placed a hand around her torso. Eleanor opened her eyes and smiled at the sight of Rebecca. ***"Good morning my love."***

"Good morning. What time is it?" Rebecca could now escape from the covers. *"It's 6 am. and look…. the sun is out."* Eleanor turned slightly towards the window as if to validate Rebecca's statement. Eleanor fluffed some pillows as she propped herself up. *"So…how are you feeling?"* Rebecca stroked Eleanor's face as she answered. *"I'm fine but my body is reminding me of yesterdays exercise. How about you? How is your wound?"* Eleanor got up and put on her robe. The slight twinge that Rebecca saw answered her question yet Eleanor was not about to admit to such pain. *"Fine."* She went to the window and gazed cautiously out of it. Rebecca stood behind Eleanor as she spoke. *"I thought you promised not to lie to me?"* Eleanor turned to face her. *"What are you talking about?"* Rebecca reached down and untied Eleanor's robe. *"I'm talking about this."* She placed her hands gently on Eleanor's wound and Eleanor doubled over in pain. *"You are in pain yet you won't even be truthful with me. Why?"* Eleanor looked at her with tears in her eyes. *"I'm not use to letting my feelings show. It's been a sign of weakness. Besides, you would only feel more guilty."* *"Don't try to side track the conversation. I want you to get that treated immediately!"* Rebecca then stormed into her room and began to dress. Eleanor decided to do the same.

Both women were quiet as the walked downstairs towards the lobby. Eleanor received a note from her brother stating that Mr. Doyle was on his way to Waverly Manor to speak with her.

She looked at her pocket watch and realized the hour had come. *"We have time for some breakfast if you like."* Rebecca said as she picked up her falling notes. Eleanor wished she could stay but wasn't sure of the issue with Mr. Doyle. *"Actually, I have to return to Waverly Manor. I have someone on their way to see me regarding Mr. Randhorne. If I am to make it, I need to leave now. I'm sorry."* Rebecca looked worried. She remembered Eleanor mentioning the officious little man and the potential problem he could pose for Eleanor. *"Will you be alright?" "Yes…I'll be fine. And don't worry, I'll have Dr. Graves look at my injury."* She nodded as Eleanor gave her an acceptable hug. Before she could question her further, she was out the inn door.

Once at the manor Eleanor informed Mrs. Potter of Mr. Doyle's impending arrival and her retirement to the library. Eleanor would calm her thoughts and try to focus on the matters at hand. She poured a small glass of whiskey, and selected Alfred Lord Tennyson's *In Memoriam* to read. As she read Locksley Hall, Tennyson's problems of religious faith, political power and social change seemed to mirror some of her struggles. She sent for Dr. Graves as she had promised Rebecca. Mrs. Potter entered the library with the post and informed Eleanor that the bridge was out and that travel to the city would be delayed. Eleanor was relieved since she knew it would take Mr. Doyle a few days to arrive. She fell asleep on the couch in front of the fireplace.

The next morning, she went up to her room, dressed and headed to breakfast. She listened to the local gossip of the servants and decided to head back to the library. She missed Rebecca and her energy. She decided today she would re-read Charles Dickens *David Copperfield*. Once again, she poured herself a drink. As she sipped the amber liquid the sound of an arriving carriage was heard. Within a few minutes Mrs. Potter knocked at the library door announcing Mr. Doyle. *"Lady Heddington......my name is Cedric Doyle and I am from Thackeray, Austen and Thackeray Purveyors."* He handed her his card and sat down. Eleanor was shocked yet remained calm. This man was no official but merely a business agent for a company. Eleanor knew that many people tried to get an audience with E.B. Randhorne but never to the point of such tenacity. *"Yes.... Mr. Doyle...what can I do for you?"* *"My company is...."* A frantic knock came at the door. Mrs. Potter opened it with a newspaper in one hand and a tissue in the other. *"Mrs. Potter? What is it?"* She handed her mistress the paper. There on the front page was the headline: **E.B. Randhorne Lost at Sea: Jade Starr Sinks off English Coast**. Eleanor was stunned as she starred at the paper. *"Mr. Doyle, I think it is better that you conduct this business with Mr. Randhorne's solicitor. I'm sorry... you must forgive me."* Eleanor ran upstairs to her room and closed the door. She watched as Mrs. Potter ushered Mr. Doyle down the front steps and into an awaiting carriage.

Meanwhile, back at the Westmore ruins Rebecca studied the aftermath of yesterdays storm. But much to her surprise the rain had helped to uncover more of the stone wall and the mysterious Celtic cross. Most of her students had recovered the artifacts that seemed to wash towards the cross and tents were repositioned once again. Courtney Adams ran up to Rebecca nearly running her over. ***"Professor! Have you seen the headlines of this mornings paper?"*** The young woman held it up for Rebecca. Her heart sank. She knew who E.B. Randhorne really was. so how could this be? She grabbed the paper from the young woman and feverishly began to read the story of the Jade Starr and how E.B. Randhorne was to sail to the Americas to further his investments on this ship he had just purchased. On its way to Spain it hit a small reef off the coast of England and sank with only 5 survivors, all of which were the crew. Each gave a heroic account of E.B. Randhorne saving them and then being trapped by the collapsing mast.

Rebecca tried to see when the Jade Starr had left. Did Rebecca have enough time to get on the ship? Mrs. Potter would know. Rebecca left the dig in senior university student Courtney Adams hands while she made arrangements to get a carriage. She packed her notes and sketches of the dig so she could get caught up on her report to the university. She then realized that Mary Masterson's Horseless Carriage would be faster. Once she located the student the two women were off to Waverly Manor.

Eleanor sent word to her solicitor regarding E.B. Randhorne's death and knew that there would be documents and papers to sign within the next few weeks. She also sent word to her brother that she needed to speak with him as soon as possible. She had thought about turning over the business to him before but now it would be a necessity since Victorian manner dictated that a man would have to run such a complicated and large business. Technically, nothing would change except for E.B. Randhorne's generous estate going to Eleanor and his presence, as it were, in the public's eye. Eleanor would still make the decisions as she always did. Even now wreaths and condolences started to arrive. Mrs. Potter cleaned out a section of the old study to start housing the gifts and mail. Eleanor decided to settle back down to the library and sat in front of the fireplace. She dozed off gazing into the fire.

Rebecca thanked Mary Masterson and sent her back to the Westmore dig. Rebecca ran up the stone stairs and knocked frantically on the front door. When no one answered she opened it and walked quickly down the hall calling for Mrs. Potter. She instinctively ran into the library as Eleanor was getting out of the chair. *"Rebecca? What are you doing here? What's all the commotion?"* Eleanor desperately tried to wipe the sleep from her eyes as she stood in front of Rebecca. She was suddenly engulfed in Rebecca's arms. Eleanor remained still as her mind desperately tried to awaken. Rebecca held Eleanor at arms length as if she were to scold her. *"Haven't you read the papers? You're.... I mean E.B. is dead!" "Yes.... I know."* Rebecca sat down as if she had been punched. *"I thought you were on that ship. I thought you were....... dead."* Rebecca began to cry. Eleanor closed her eyes not realizing what Rebecca would have thought about the demise of Randhorne. She knelt down in front of Rebecca and gently held her hand. *"My love.... I am truly sorry. I had no idea that you would make that type of connection. I would have sent you a note. I am so sorry."* She sat on the edge of the chair and hugged the sobbing woman. She reached behind her and grabbed the drink she had started. *"Here...drink this."* Rebecca drank the liquid and it seemed to steady her nerves. *"I can't take much more of this. First, I thought I had lost you with your encounter with the highway man. Then I thought I would die in that mudslide and never be able to tell you how much I loved you, and now almost losing you again on a sinking ship?"* Eleanor tried not to laugh but Rebecca's way of recounting the events made her stifle her amusement. She then realized that Rebecca said she loved her. *"You know.... there is only one way in which this dilemma can be solved."* Eleanor whispered gently in her ear. Rebecca looked at her as she dried her eyes. *"What?"* Eleanor stood up and leaned on the mantle of the fireplace. She waited and then turned to face Rebecca. *"Lady Eleanor Heddington is going to need someone to help her through this stressful, upsetting time since her boss has passed away. I'm sure your moving in would be most appropriate and she could travel with you once you went back to the university. After all, two women traveling is certainly better than one, at least according to Mr. Brumby."* Eleanor watched as she waited for a reaction. She could see Rebecca processing the suggestion. She then stood up and turned to Eleanor. *"Are you really sure of this? I feel I'm always making you angry and I don't know why."* Eleanor moved in close to her. *"Please understand.... I have based my life around a lie and to keep that lie I have had to live alone to perpetuate that lie. I thought I had lost the ability to let someone in, to trust someone....to love someone. You breathed life into my existence. You don't make me angry. You make me face my own reality and there are times I don't like what I see. But the love I have for you makes me deal with it, accept it and occasionally try to change it. I can only hope that I do something for you other than make you frustrated."* Rebecca was moved by the honesty in Eleanor's words. The love she felt for Eleanor was strong and her whole being felt empty when she was not around. *"How can I tell you how much you mean to me? How can I tell you of the emptiness I feel when you are not near? How can I tell you of the passion that consumes me when your body is near? Yes.... I would consider it an honor to help Lady Heddington in her hour of need. I will make the necessary arrangements at the university regarding my schedule and I can forward my finished report to them after I have wrapped up things at the excavation site."* Both women hugged as they thought about the commitment, they had just made to one another. Each was confident with the new adventure that was about to begin.

Printed in the United States
By Bookmasters